Mr. Magic

The Would-Be Wizard

FROM IHOR
I dedicate this book to:
Kiki
for all her love and inspiration
and
to Alex, my nephew
and
Tommy, my godson
and
especially to
Joyce
for bringing Mr. Magic to life

FROM JOYCE
Thanks to Ihor, Roxy, Kiki, Kenny & Gary for tolerating my "abuse" and yet (still!) not ceasing to care and support.

Thanks also to Charles Lamar for his helpful criticism as well as C. Donna and C. Raciti.

MR. MAGIC
THE WOULD-BE WIZARD
Text Copyright © 1987 by IHOR
Illustrations Copyright © 1987 by JOYCE HARADA
All rights reserved
First Edition Published 1987.
Mechanicals by Rhino Graphics, Kauai
Published by ELFWORKS PRESS, P.O. 699 Anahola, HI 96703
Library of Congress Catalog Number 87-80768
I.S.B.N. 0-940765-01-2

Printed in Hong Kong

Mr. Magic

The Would-Be Wizard

By

Ihor

Illustrations by

Joyce Harada

ELFWORKS

P. O. Box 699, Anahola, Kauai, HI 96703

It started as a whisper
On a warm and starry night,
Behind the hollow tringle tree
Just hidden out of sight.
When Mr. Magic looked around
And clambered to the top,
He couldn't find a single thing;
The whisper didn't stop.

As he climbed down, he checked each branch
For birds who'd come to stay,
Then felt under the flower beds
Where field mice liked to play.
And when he'd searched all 'round and 'round
But couldn't find a thing,
The whisper stopped, then laughed a laugh,
And soon began to sing.

"I like to ride a comet's tail
When traveling to a star.
I like to tickle sleeping fish,
With moonbeams, from afar.
But most of all I like to sing
To bid the night goodbye,
Then slide down rainbows, through the dawn,
And kiss the blushing sky."

This startled Mr. Magic so,
He jumped and tried to hide.
But as his hat was much too large,
He disappeared inside.
His purple socks and button shoes
Were all that one could see,
While almost all the rest of him
Was hidden comfortably.

"If someone, please," He shouted out,
"Extracts me from my brim,
Then any treasure I possess
I'll gladly give to him."
But as he spoke, and took a breath,
Some dust flew up his nose.
He paused...then snoze a mighty sneeze
And through the air he rose.

Head over heels he whirled around,
"Look out below," he said.
And though he flapped his arms to stop,
He landed on his head.
He blinked his eyes, still upside-down,
And cried, "Is someone there?"
When out of darkness, there appeared,
A glitter in the air.

A laughing girl with clear blue eyes
Came through this sparkling light,
All dressed in gold with diamond wings
That glistened in the night.
The shimmer vanished...then she spoke
In that familiar voice.
"Why are you standing on your head?
It seems an oddly choice!"

"My name is Starlight," laughed the girl,
"You really needn't frown
Because I played a joke on you,
That popped you upside-down.
Here let me help you...won't you, sir?"
She said, and gave her hand.
"The world's a more familiar place
When on your feet you stand."

"No thank you!" Mr. Magic hruumphed,
"I'll do it on my own.
You've done enough...you nincompoop!"
He used a nasty tone.
But as he tried to bend his legs
To get them on the ground
He teeter-tottered, then he fell
And made an oooffing sound.

As Starlight watched him lie quite still,
All crumpled in a heap,
She thought perhaps he'd hurt himself
Or maybe fell asleep.
But suddenly. . .up straight he sat
And quickly looked around.
He grabbed his hat, and brushed it off
. . .Then jumped up from the ground.

"Young lady!" He addressed the girl,
"It seems that you don't see,
Just who I am and what I do,
To trifle so with me.
My magic's great, my power fierce,
And all who see me quake.
To play your silly tricks on me
Is clearly a mistake!"

"For if I choose to take offense,"
He gravely said to her,
"You might end up a mugglewort
With pink and yellow fur.
Or maybe with a magic word,
I'll make you two feet tall
With leafy arms and big webbed feet
You wouldn't like at all."

"So my advice to you," he said,
While puffing out his chest,
"Is leaving well enough alone.
You'll find that would be best."
Then Starlight softly spoke to him.
She dusted off his suit.
"The reason that I joked with you
Is 'cause I think you're cute."

Then Mr. Magic blushed beet red,
And tried to look away.
He fumbled with his bindersleeve
Without a word to say.
Then slowly he turned 'round to her
To look her in the eye
And with a hiccup and a snort
He started in to cry.

"You think it's fun to laugh at me?"
He wiped away a tear.
"A wizard's very hard to be,
I've worked on it a year.
I've done my best," he said to her,
And sadly heaved a sigh.
"My magic only seems to work,
Whenever I don't try."

When Starlight heard the tearful words
That Mr. Magic said,
She didn't laugh . . . but took his hand
And winked at him instead.
"Why don't you cast your favorite spell?"
She squeezed his fingers tight.
"And I will listen to the words
To make sure they are right."

A sudden light shone in his eyes.
He gulped and bravely said,
"I know an ancient spell, you see,
That transforms gold to lead.
No! . . . That one never works too well,"
She heard him softly say,
"Those metals won't behave themselves . . .
They change the other way."

"I've got it!" Mr. Magic shrieked,
And danced a happy jig.
"I'll take a yellow daffodil
And turn it to a pig."
But then he scratched his head and cried,
"That surely can't be right.
The daffodils are sleeping now.
We won't find one at night."

"Instead," said Starlight, "let's have fun
And play a magic game.
I'll make you vanish from this place
And then I'll do the same.
We'll pop up in your hollow tree
To give the owls a scare.
And then you'll make a magic pass
To bring us both back here."

That sounded like a perfect trick,
So Starlight spoke the words,
That popped them up inside the tree
And startled all the birds.
Then Mr. Magic crossed his eyes
And hummed his magic tune.
He scratched his nose and hopped three times
Then hissed like a raccoon.

A cloudy mist formed 'round their feet
And took them by surprise.
It wisped and curled up through the air
While muffling both their cries.
They flew straight up into the sky
Much quicker than a wink.
The mist then melted all at once
And they began to sink.

When suddenly from who knows where
A giant hand appeared.
And right behind, an ancient face
With demon's teeth and beard.
What happened next was lightning fast.
The fingers opened wide
Then quickly closed around them both
And captured them inside.

"Who summons me with magic songs?"
They heard a voice intone.
"I've dreamt a whole eternity
Upon my cloudy throne."
The giant's eyes were emerald moons
With brows like white-capped seas.
"Who is so bold, that they would dare,
To call me as they please?"

Then Starlight whispered "Quite a trick,"
In Mr. Magic's ear.
"Your recitation of that spell
Was just a little queer."
"The problem, don't you see," she said,
"Is very roundabout.
The tune you sang was upside-down...
The words were inside-out."

"Speak louder!" quaked the giant voice.
"Who called me to this place?
At whose request this audience?
And why this merry chase?"
His massive brow began to knit,
His smile to disappear.
He opened up his monstrous hand
And growled, "What have we here?"

He looked at each of them in turn
And struck a thoughtful pose.
He muttered, "What a lovely girl
From wings to twinkle-toes."
"This other one," he thought out loud
"Is quite another thing."
He cleared his throat and gruffly asked,
"Which one of you did sing?"

"T'was I who 'roused you from your sleep,
Though quite by accident.
To interrupt your peaceful dreams
Was never my intent.
My name is Mr. Magic, Sir,
But I suppose I should,
Be called, by all who know me well,
As Mr. Never Could."

"My name is Golgothar, you see,
And power is my destiny.
But anyone who conquers me
Will make their wish, reality."

"Be silent, knave!" the giant growled,
"Your words are wearisome.
Do you think any simpleton
Could summon me to come?
It just so happens that you've both
Released me from a spell
That held me captive in my sleep
More years than I can tell."

With Mr. Magic's hand in hers,
Sweet Starlight strained to fly.
On diamond sparkling wings they rose
Into the endless sky.
The giant's hand closed 'round thin air.
He raged and bellowed threats.
"I'll catch you now, you little fools,
And keep you both as pets!"

So back and forth and up and down,
They darted side to side.
And dodged the mighty grasping hand
From which they couldn't hide.
Then Mr. Magic said there was
A spell he'd improvise,
To change the giant to a flea
And so, reduce his size.

Then Starlight said, "I'll call his name
To draw his gaze away.
I'll give you all the time you need
To do just as you say.
So when your magic starts to work
to make the giant small,
Then I will fly as fast as wind
and catch you as you fall."

When Starlight fluttered into view
To call the giant's name,
His hand reached out and swatted her
As if it were a game.
Then Mr. Magic shouted out
Enchanted song and verse,
But Golgothar just laughed at him,
Untouched by any curse.

The mammoth face turned up just then
To search the cloudy sky.
As Mr. Magic tumbled down,
He struck the emerald eye.
"My fatal flaw!" the giant wailed,
"You've smashed my evil eye
My power's gone, you bumbling fool!
. . .And now I shrink and die!"

Then Mr. Magic turned and saw,
That Starlight's eyes were dim.
She tumbled wildly through the air
And would not answer him.
He fought his way through wind and clouds
And clasped her to his side,
But he could not awaken her
Although he tried and tried!

"You've conquered me!...but you have lost."
He heard the giant's cry.
"As you will not survive this fall
Through miles of empty sky."
But Mr. Magic shouted out,
"Not so, you wicked ghoul.
I claim the wish that I have earned.
Don't think me such a fool."

The giant scowled and nodded back
While shrinking rapidly.
"Then quickly choose, before you die,
What is your wish to be?"
Without a pause, the answer came
In Mr. Magic's voice,
"I wish to save brave Starlight's life!
I've given you my choice."

Then suddenly a brilliant flash
With crashing, thunderous sound
Transported them on magic winds
And set them on the ground.
Sweet Starlight's eyes now opened wide.
They overflowed with love.
While on her right was Golgothar
In wizard's robe and glove.

"Your trial is done. . .now hear me well,"
The ancient wizard said,
"You've overcome the giant fiend
That filled you with such dread.
By saving Starlight, not yourself,
Your courage you've revealed.
Beyond the realm of words. . .with deeds
That cannot be concealed."

The wizard turned and looked away
While tilting up his head.
He walked to Mr. Magic's side
And then he softly said.
"The Magic born of Love endures
And will not break apart.
So always teach your mind to seek
What's written in your heart."

"And if you wish I'll take you on
As my apprentice now."
But Mr. Magic couldn't speak
. . . He'd quite forgotten how.
Then Golgothar raised up his arms.
He winked and pulled his beard.
And when sweet Starlight kissed them both
They simply disappeared.

The End